D1576193

DARK MAN

DANGER IN THE DARK

by Peter Lancett

illustrated by Jan Pedroietta

SADDLEBACK
EDUCATIONAL PUBLISHING

DARK MAN

Danger in the Dark
The Dark Dreams
The Dark Glass
The Dark Side of Magic
The Dark Waters of Time
The Shadow in the Dark

David Strachan, The Old Man and The Shadow Masters appear
by kind permission of Peter Lancett

This edition is published by arrangement with Ransom Publishing Ltd.

SADDLEBACK
EDUCATIONAL PUBLISHING
www.sdlback.com

ISBN-13: 978-1-61651-016-9
ISBN-10: 1-61651-016-1

Printed in Guangzhou, China
1110/11-03-10

15 14 13 12 11 2 3 4 5 6 7

Chapter One:
The Girl

The Dark Man is not alone.

The girl is with him.

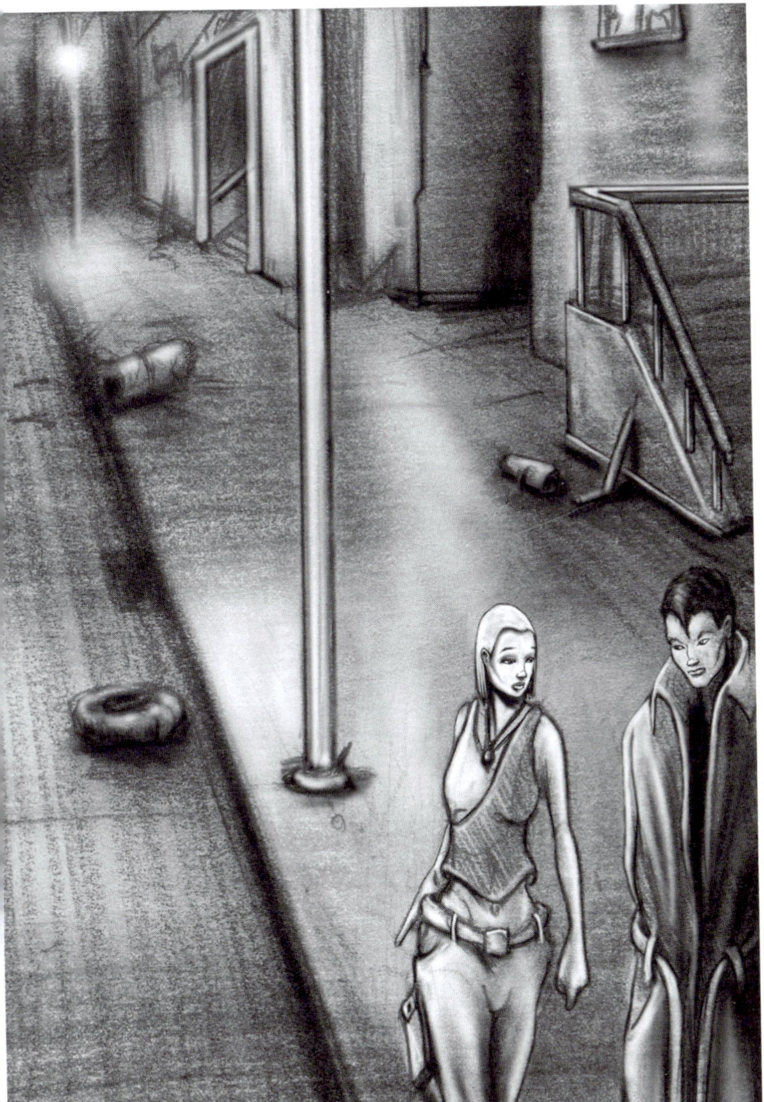

They are walking in the bad part of the city at night.

The Dark Man has found her.

He must take her to the Old Man.

The Old Man is in a safe place.

Chapter Two:
Demons on the Streets

The girl is very scared.

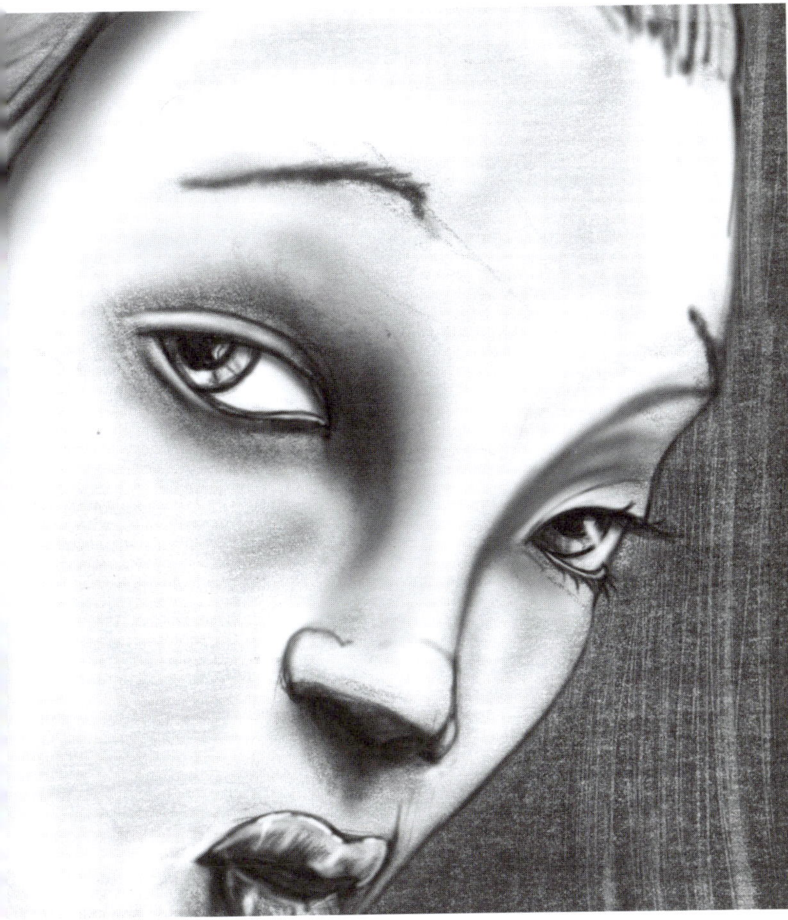

The Shadow Masters want to find her.

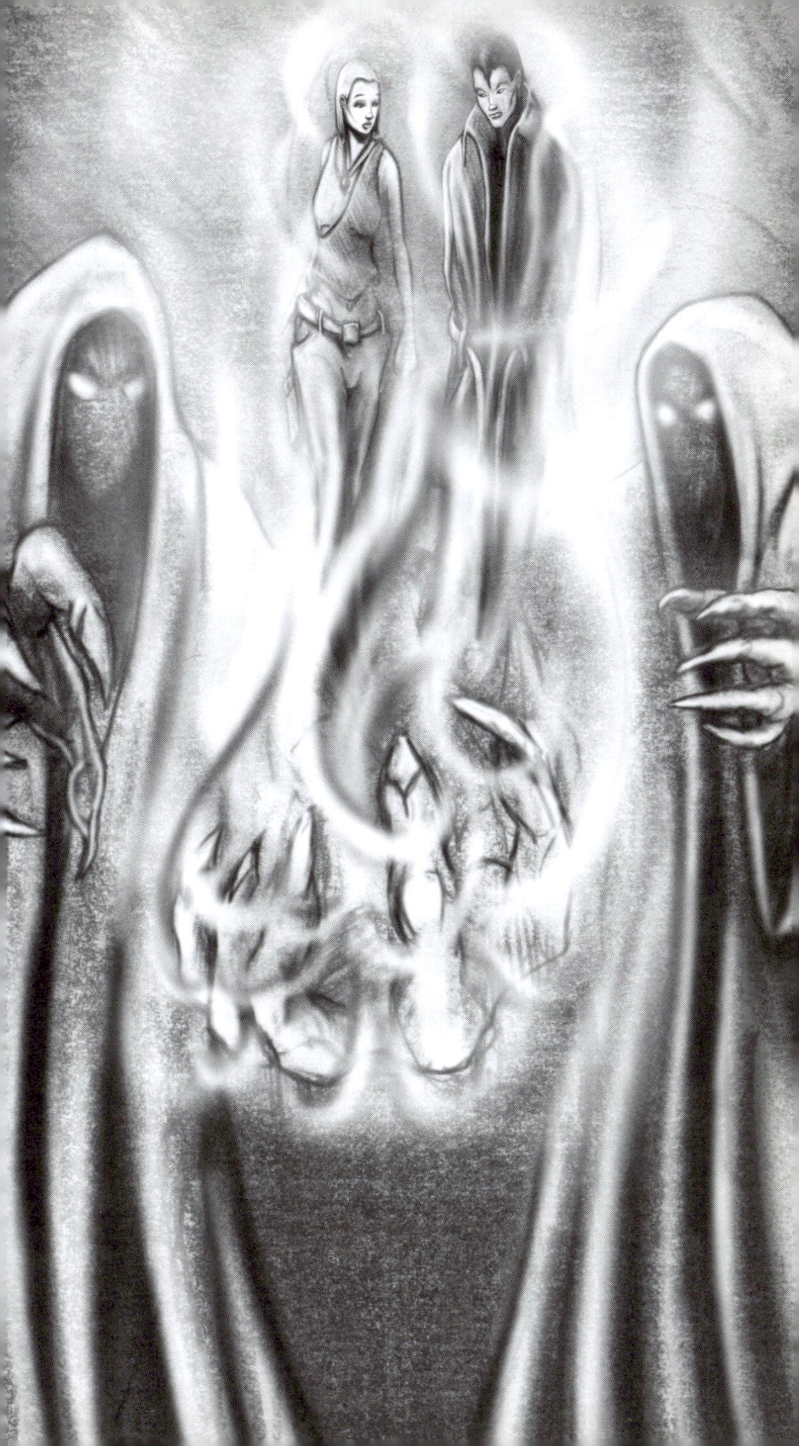

She has a secret power.

The Shadow Masters will use her to find a magic stone.

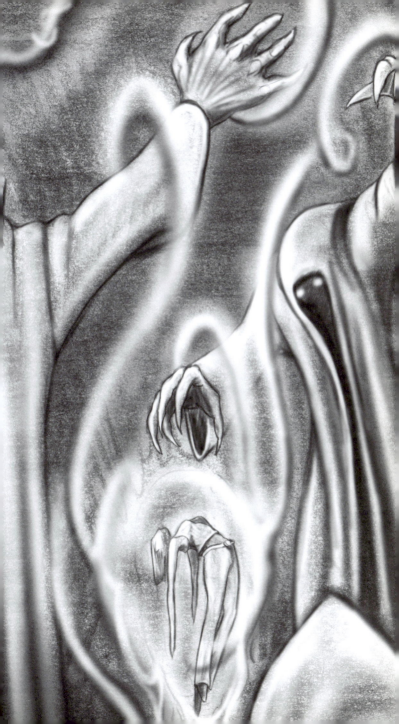

Because it is night, they have put demons on the streets.

The demons can look like men.

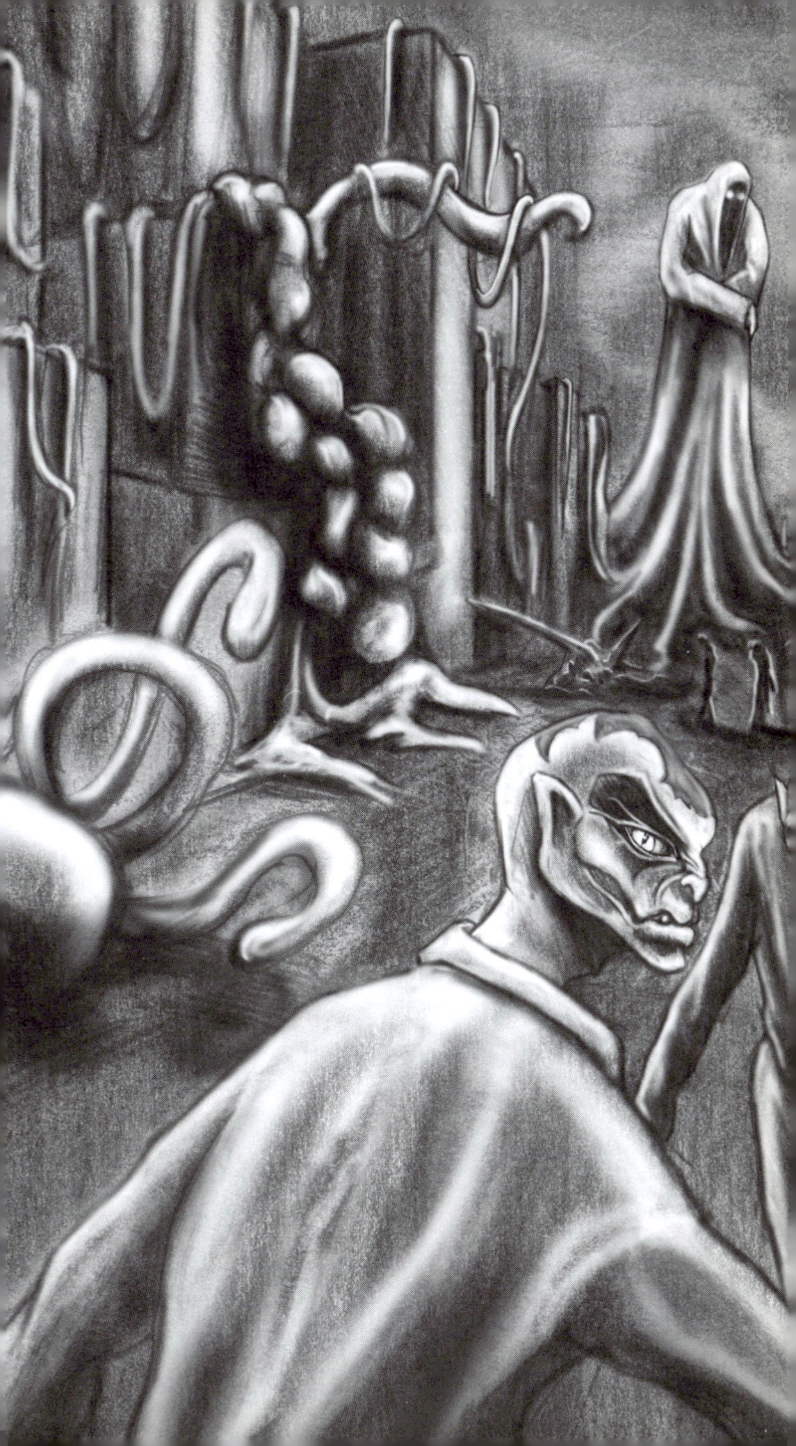

Chapter Three:
The Dog

A dog comes around a corner.

The Dark Man stops and the girl hides
behind him.

She holds his coat.

The dog could be a demon.

Demons have come in the shape of animals before.

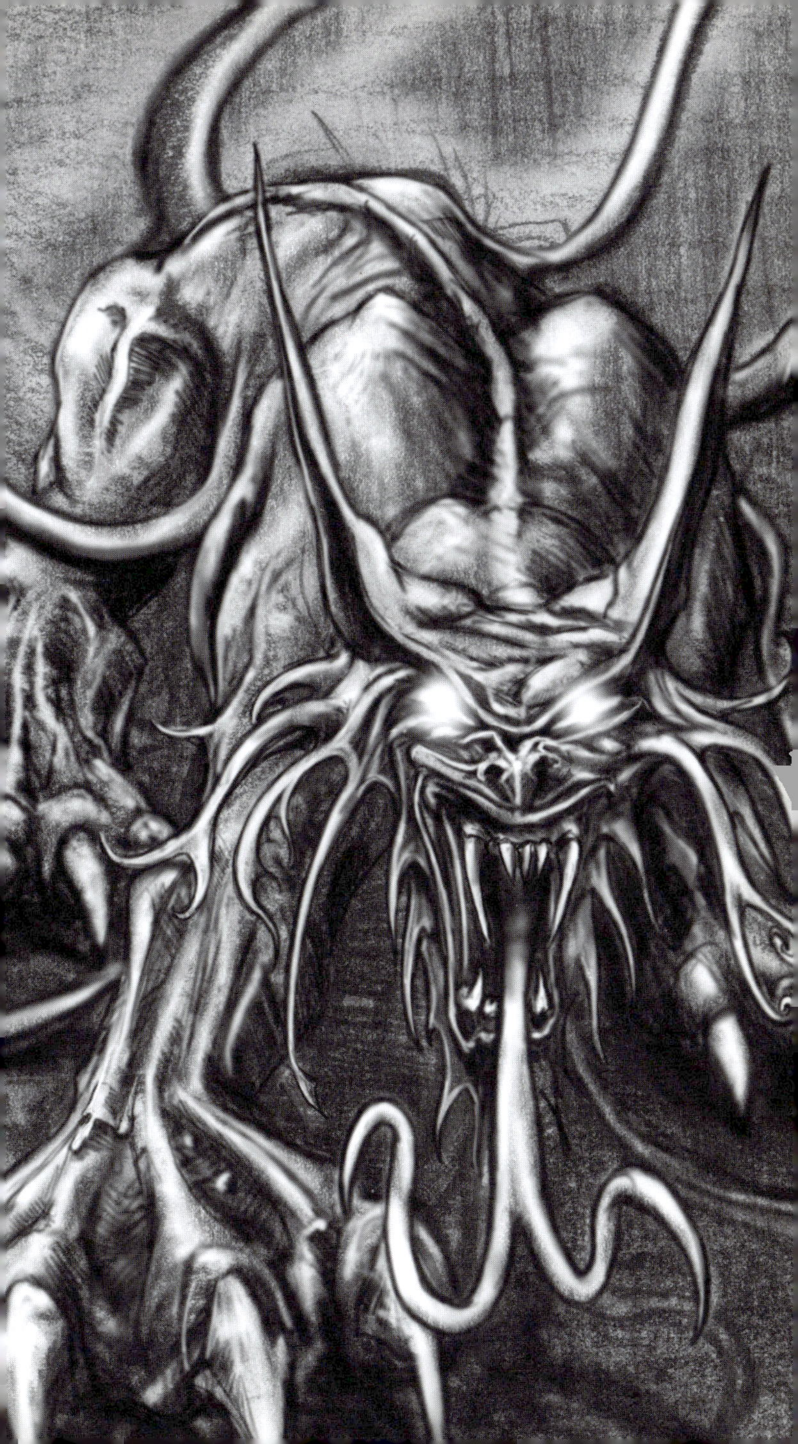

This dog just walks across the road.

Chapter Four:
Danger in the Dark

The Dark Man and the girl walk on.

Now they can see the lights in the good part of the city.

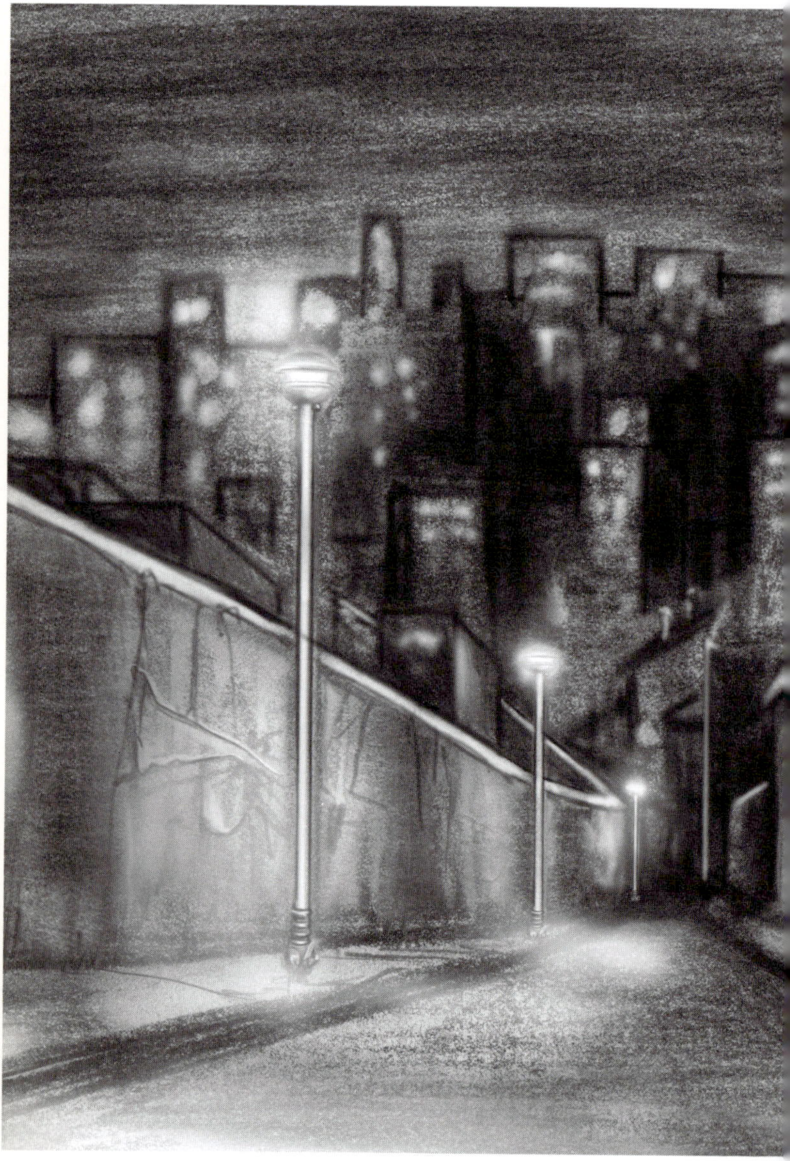

THE AUTHOR

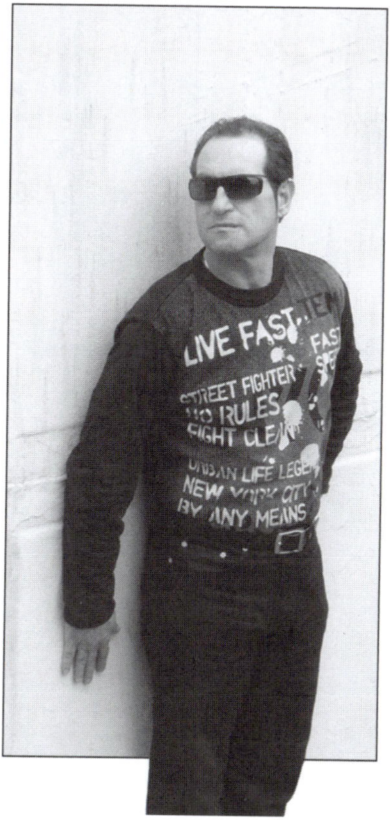
LIVE FAST
STREET FIGHTER
RULES

photograph: Rachel Ottewill

Peter Lancett used to work in the movies. Then he worked in the city. Now he writes horror stories for a living. "It beats having a proper job," he says.

Soon they will be at the place where the Old Man waits.

The Dark Man cannot feel safe.

The streets here are still dark.

There are shadows all around.

There are dark doorways where demons can hide.

Soon they will be safe, but the Dark Man
does not rest.

It is dark.

There is always danger in the dark.

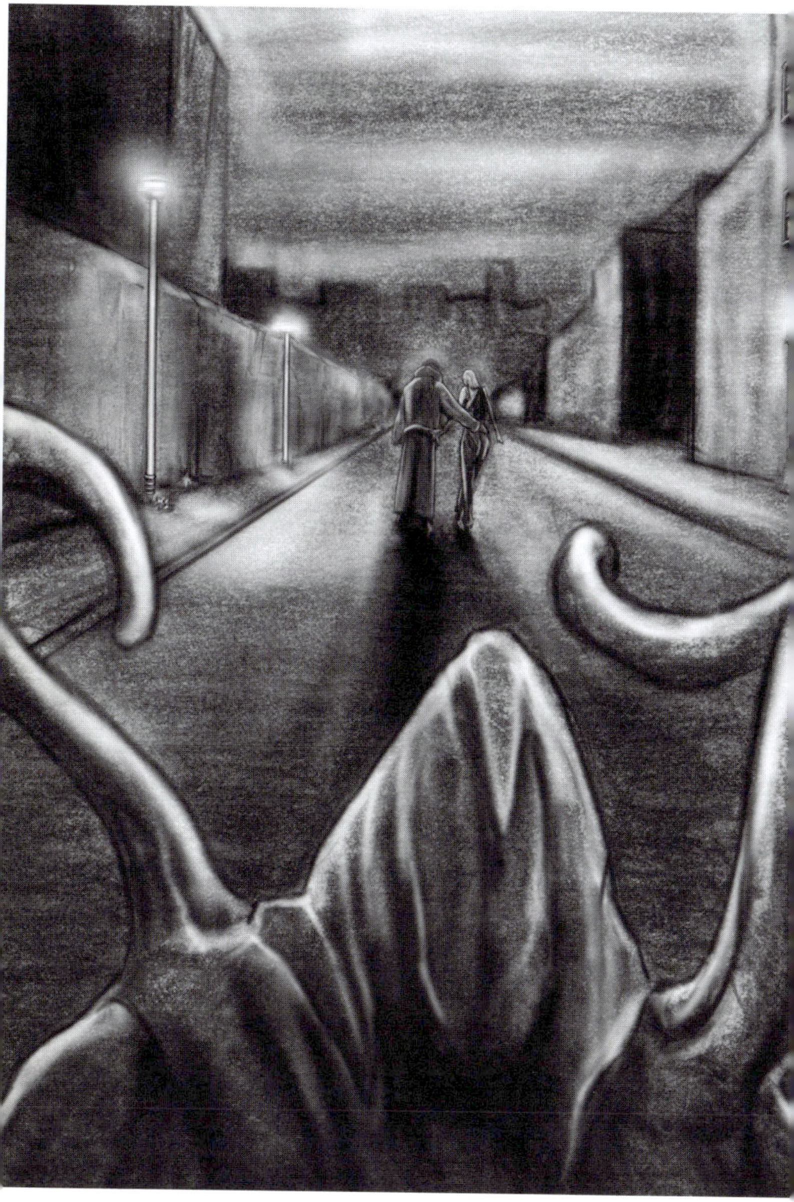